PRIMARY SOURCES IN AMERICAN HISTORY™

ELLIS ISLAND

A PRIMARY SOURCE HISTORY OF AN
IMMIGRANT'S ARRIVAL IN AMERICA

GILLIAN HOUGHTON

rosen central
Primary Source™

The Rosen Publishing Group, Inc., New York

For Trip and Gordo

Published in 2004 by The Rosen Publishing Group, Inc.
29 East 21st Street, New York, NY 10010

Copyright © 2004 by The Rosen Publishing Group, Inc.

First Edition

Library of Congress Cataloging-in-Publication Data

Houghton, Gillian.
Ellis Island: a primary source history of an immigrant's arrival in America/
Gillian Houghton.
    p. cm. — (Primary sources in American history)
Summary: Primary sources bring to life the immigrant experience through a history of America's most famous point of entry, Ellis Island.
Includes bibliographical references and index.
ISBN 0-8239-4003-9 (library binding)
1. Ellis Island Immigration Station (N.Y. and N.J.)—History—Sources—
Juvenile literature. 2. United States—Emigration and immigration—History—
Sources—Juvenile literature. 3. United States—Emigration and
immigration—Government policy—History—Sources—Juvenile literature.
[1. Ellis Island Immigration Station (N.Y. and N.J.)—History—Sources.
2. United States—Emigration and immigration—History—Sources.]
I. Title. II. Series.
JV6484.H68 2004
304.8'73—dc21

2003001081

Manufactured in the United States of America

On the front cover: A photograph entitled *New York, Ellis Island*. Courtesy of the Library of Congress.

On the back cover: First row (left to right): immigrants arriving at Ellis Island; Generals Lee and Grant meet to discuss terms of Confederate surrender at Appomattox, Virginia. Second row (left to right): Lewis and Clark meeting with a western Native American tribe during the expedition of the Corps of Discovery; Napoléon at the signing of the Louisiana Purchase. Third row (left to right): Cherokee traveling along the Trail of Tears during their forced relocation west of the Mississippi River; escaped slaves traveling on the Underground Railroad.

CONTENTS

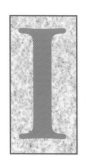NTRODUCTION

> Give me your tired, your poor,
> Your huddled masses yearning to breathe free,
> The wretched refuse of your teeming shore.
> Send these, the homeless, tempest-tost to me,
> I lift my lamp beside the golden door!
> —Emma Lazarus, "The New Colossus"

THE GOLDEN DOOR

Throughout the nineteenth and twentieth centuries, millions of people from every country in the world heard the call of freedom and opportunity expressed in Emma Lazarus's famous poem, "The New Colossus," which is engraved on the pedestal of the Statue of Liberty and greets every visitor to New York Harbor. The promise it extended led hopeful and often desperate travelers to leave their homes and immigrate to the United States. The single largest port of entry for these prospective Americans was New York Harbor. From 1892 to 1954, the federal immigration station through which they were required to pass was Ellis Island.

In the hundred-year period between 1820 and 1920, about 25.5 million immigrants settled permanently in the United States, with 12 million of them passing through Ellis Island. When the arrivals to New York Harbor boarded the ferries and barges that connected Ellis Island to lower Manhattan, they joined and forever changed the fabric of the American experience.

Ellis Island, New York City.

During its peak years, 1892 to 1924, the immigration center at Ellis Island *(shown above)* greeted and processed thousands of immigrants a day. Today, over 100 million Americans have an ancestor who took a great leap into the unknown, left his or her native land, sailed to America, and passed through the "golden door" of Ellis Isand.

Immigration continues to be a vibrant force in American culture today, even though, as in the earliest days of Ellis Island, the government's immigration policies are fiercely debated. Consider Miami's Little Haiti and Little Havana; the Islamic community of Dearborn, Michigan; San Francisco's Chinatown; or the Greek community of Astoria, Queens. These vital communities are the products of America's long history of immigration, each one of them representing a different era in our shared past. An examination of the history of Ellis Island reveals the origins of American diversity and offers a powerful and moving account of the immigrant experience.

TIMELINE

1807 — The family of Samuel Ellis sells what will become known as Ellis Island to New York State.

1808 — The U.S. government buys the island from New York State for $10,000.

1813 — Fort Gibson is built on the island, housing a large store of ammunition.

1861 — Fort Gibson is dismantled. Ellis Island becomes the land's official name.

1890 — Ellis Island is chosen as the site for a new federal immigration station for the port of New York.

1892 — The Ellis Island Immigration Center opens on January 1.

1897 — The wooden immigration buildings of Ellis Island are destroyed by fire.

1900 — The Ellis Island Immigration Center reopens. The new buildings are made of brick and stone.

TIMELINE

1907 —— More people immigrate to the United States than in any other year. Roughly 1.3 million immigrants pass through Ellis Island.

1924 —— Immigration through Ellis Island begins to wane.

1943 —— Ellis Island is transformed into a detention center for prisoners of war and aliens.

1954 —— Ellis Island is closed.

1965 —— President Lyndon Johnson makes Ellis Island a part of the National Park Service.

1974 —— The Restore Ellis Island Committee is formed to raise money for renovations.

1983 —— Restoration on Ellis Island's main building begins.

1990 —— The Ellis Island Immigration Museum opens on September 10.

1998 —— The U.S. Supreme Court rules that most of Ellis Island falls within the borders of New Jersey, not New York.

CHAPTER 1

When, in the early 1660s, the first Dutch colonists arrived in New Amsterdam (later to be renamed New York after the colony was acquired by England), the future Ellis Island was just a muddy three-acre sandbank barely rising above the waters of the harbor during high tide. It was notable only for its rich oyster beds and for the schools of shad (a fish related to the herring) that swam past its shores. Ships could not dock in the shallow water that surrounded it. Little vegetation grew on its higher ground. The island was not of much interest to anybody.

A SANDBANK IN THE HARBOR

An Island's Humble Beginnings

In the course of its unimpressive early history, the island was known variously as Dyre's Island, Bucking Island, Gibbet Island, and Oyster Island. It gained its modern name from Samuel Ellis, the island's only known eighteenth-century owner, who bought the property sometime before 1785. When Ellis died in 1794, the island was willed to a grandson, who soon died as well. Ownership of the property passed among the members of the Ellis family for the following decade. Though privately owned, the island had become home to a small army battery (a fort housing artillery pieces, such as cannons, that were used to defend the surrounding land and waterways).

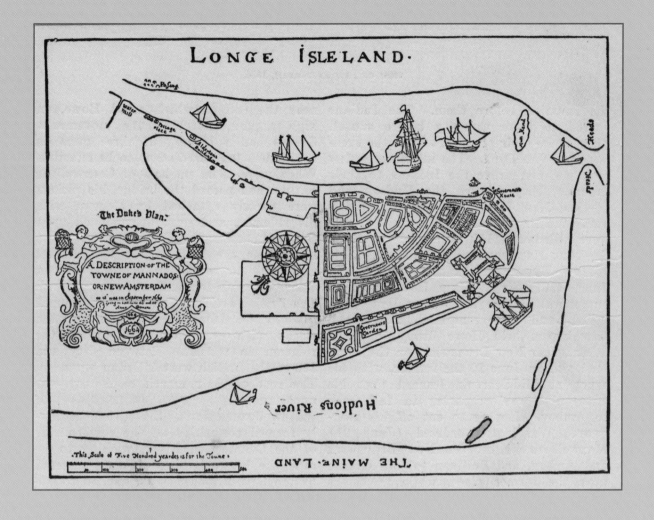

This is a 1664 map entitled *The Duke's Plan: A Description of the Towne of Mannados or New Amsterdam*. It was presented to James, duke of York, shortly after the English captured the city from the Dutch and renamed it after the duke. James would later become James II, king of England. It is probably based on a 1661 map made for Dutch authorities by Jacques Cortelyou. The sharp vertical line that forms the northern boundary of the densely settled portion of Manhattan Island indicates the wall that used to defend the city from attacks. It has long since disappeared. In its place—and named after it—is Wall Street, the famous thoroughfare of international finance. Ellis Island is the thin strip of land in red at the bottom right corner of the map.

In 1794, with the threat of war with France looming, the United States government sought to construct a series of defensive fortifications in New York Harbor. The army's chief of engineers chose Ellis Island, along with neighboring Bedloe's and Governor's Islands, as the main sites of military operations. Construction of defensive works proceeded on the island over the next decade. In 1807, the state of New York began proceedings to purchase the island from the Ellis family for military purposes. Having acquired it, New York deeded the property to the federal government the following year.

While military construction proceeded on Bedloe's and Governor's Islands, sandy terrain prevented the building of anything substantial on Ellis Island. The army's original plans were scrapped. Instead, it built a small battery with room for only twenty guns, which was completed just before the outbreak of the War of 1812. During this conflict between the United States and Great Britain, Ellis Island supported a small garrison (a military post housing troops) but saw no active combat.

The following decades were uneventful on Ellis Island. It was occasionally used as the site of executions and as an army recruitment depot until 1835, when the U.S. Navy occupied the island and installed a powder magazine (a storage facility for thousands of barrels of gunpowder). This arsenal was handed over to the U.S. Army, when that branch of the military was given control of the island in 1841. A small navy guard, however, continued to protect and maintain the magazine over the next three decades. Additional defensive works were constructed during the Civil War, and the stockpile of weapons and gunpowder grew. At the end of the war and again several years later, public outcry arose over the possible dangers of such a large quantity of explosive material gathered in a

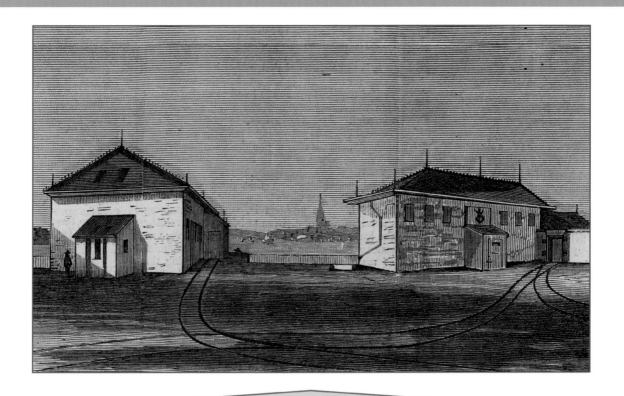

This is an 1868 sketch of the United States Navy powder magazines on Ellis Island. These buildings housed artillery shells and gunpowder. The structure on the right once served as officers' quarters and barracks before being converted into a shell house. Fort Gibson stood just to the right of these buildings. Manhattan can be seen in the distance, with the spire of Trinity Church the tallest visible structure in the picture's center background.

place so close to the densely populated metropolitan centers of New York City and Jersey City, New Jersey. Nothing was done about it, however, until 1890, when ever-growing waves of immigration aroused a new interest in the possible usefulness of the muddy strip of unfertile land that was Ellis Island.

Ellis Island's Predecessor

Since 1855, New York City had welcomed its new immigrants at Castle Garden on the Battery in lower Manhattan, where a staff of state employees recorded their arrivals. Beginning in 1875, however, the federal government began taking a more active role in regulating and overseeing immigration. That year several nationwide immigration laws were enacted, aimed primarily at excluding criminals and prostitutes. Additional legislation in 1882 expanded the list of undesirable immigrants to include "any convict, lunatic, idiot, or any person unable to take care of himself or herself without becoming a public charge" (as quoted in Thomas Monroe Pitkin's *Keeper of the Gate*). Another law passed the same year—the Chinese Exclusion Act—excluded Chinese laborers who were thought to be stealing jobs from American workers. In 1885, the Alien Contract Labor Law was passed in order to protect the jobs and wages of American workers. It forbade American employers from recruiting foreign workers (who were willing to work for low wages) and paying for their passage.

Along with the U.S. government's new involvement in immigration policy came the creation of a federally structured immigration system. The secretary of the U.S. Treasury, in cooperation with state officials, was given the responsibility of enforcing immigration law and overseeing the state employees. When the state commissioners at Castle Garden failed to enforce the law, federal labor inspectors had to be stationed there to insure compliance, further cementing the joint federal-state system of immigration regulation that was developing in New York.

Nearly as soon as this federal-state system was up and running, it became the target of angry newspaper editorials and a major source of embarrassment for the Treasury Department. In 1888, Congress created a committee to look into the management of the nation's immigration stations, specifically New York's Castle Garden, through which the majority of the country's immigrants

This is a circa 1869 print showing the Barge Office of Castle Garden at the Battery section of lower Manhattan. Castle Garden was once known as the Southwest Battery and, later, Castle Clinton. It was one of more than a dozen forts built to defend New York Harbor at the time of the War of 1812. The army vacated Castle Clinton in 1821, and the city took over the property. In the summer of 1824, a new restaurant and entertainment center opened at the site, now renamed Castle Garden. A roof was added in the 1840s, and an opera house and theater operated there until 1854. On August 3, 1855, Castle Garden opened as an immigration center. During the next thirty-four years, more than 8 million people entered the United States through Castle Garden, until it was closed on April 18, 1890.

passed. That year, 546,889 immigrants landed in the United States; of that number, 418,423 landed at the port of New York. Following the congressional investigation, the inspectors at Castle Garden were accused of emotionally and physically abusing the immigrants and extorting money from them. In addition, inspectors were failing to properly enforce federal immigration laws by allowing unfit immigrants entry into the United States.

Only a few months later, after another investigation into the Castle Garden immigration office revealed serious examples of mismanagement and corruption, the secretary of the treasury ended the arrangement between the federal and state immigration commissioners. The federal government, represented by the treasury secretary, would now have sole responsibility for processing immigrants at Castle Garden.

One of the treasury secretary's first decisions was to build an immigration station in New York City large enough to handle the ever increasing number of immigrants flocking to America through New York Harbor. The treasury secretary proposed Bedloe's Island (the planned home of the Statue of Liberty, now known as Liberty Island) as the new site. The *New York World* responded to the secretary's proposal with an angry editorial. The influential and popular newspaper argued that the island, which "was to have been made into a beautiful park as a fit setting for the great Statue," would "be converted instead into a Babel," the chaotic biblical city in which the people suddenly began to speak many different languages and were no longer able to understand each other (according to Pitkin's *Keepers of the Gate*).

A later editorial in the same newspaper argued that the idea of an immigration station on "Liberty Island" was "universally deprecated [disapproved of] by those who look with pride upon Liberty's imposing beacon," as quoted by Pitkin. Americans, though fiercely proud of their shared history of liberty and equality, were wary of the growing tide of eastern and southern European immigrants, people believed to be of lesser "quality" than the earlier waves of northern and western European immigrants. The *World*'s editorials accurately reflected the odd mix of patriotism and nativism (a favoring of earlier settlers over recent immigrants) that gripped many Americans in the late 1880s.

In the wake of this controversy, Congress decided to create a temporary committee to visit New York and find a solution to the problem of the future location of the federal immigration station. Faced with the pleas of army and navy men stationed at Governor's Island to protect the arsenal there, the outcry of the *World* and similar public voices against the use of Bedloe's Island, and the congressional movement to remove the powder magazine from Ellis Island, the decision seemed clear. In spite of strong opposition from the secretary of the treasury, the committee soon voted to accept Ellis Island as New York's new immigration center. A humble plot of land that had long been considered almost useless was about to become the principal gateway to America.

CHAPTER 2

THE GATE IS OPENED

Construction on Ellis Island began in the spring of 1890, and was not completed until January 1892. The channel was dredged, and wells were dug. Soil and gravel used as ballast (a stabilizing weight) in the hulls of ships in New York Harbor were removed and used as landfill to increase the island's size from 3.3 to 27.5 acres. Some historians believe that the earth removed while building New York's subway system was also dumped into New York Harbor to help build up Ellis Island. More than 850 feet (259 meters) of docks were built, along with a large two-story main building, separate hospital buildings, a boiler house, a laundry facility, bathhouses, and an electric plant, all made of wood.

A New Immigration Center with New Policies

As Ellis Island was under construction, so too was a new legislative framework for processing immigrants and keeping out the "undesirable element," which was increasingly described in ethnic terms. Hungarians, Lithuanians, Russians (especially Russian Jews fleeing the oppression of the dictatorial czar), and Italians were believed to be ignorant, socially backward, and strange looking when compared to the British, German, and Scandinavian immigrants who came to America just a generation before.

Ethnic prejudice was not the only reason for the new immigrants' hostile reception in the United States. The more established

At top is a circa 1891 drawing of the original Ellis Island Immigration Station. The drawing and the photograph it was based on would have been completed several months before Ellis Island actually opened and began accepting immigrant arrivals on January 1, 1892. At bottom is a photograph of construction workers building one of the island's structures. The building was constructed entirely of wood, was three stories high, and was designed to handle up to 10,000 immigrants a day.

northern European immigrants feared the arrival of a labor force willing to work for less than they were. This would decrease the number of jobs available and drive down wages. In 1891, Congress passed new immigration legislation in response to the complaints of the Knights of Labor, among other nativist labor organizations. Its restrictive provisions were designed to stem the tide of immigration, thereby protecting Americans' jobs. The law placed immigration at all ports of entry entirely under federal control. It required steamship companies to transport, at the company's expense, any immigrants rejected by U.S. immigration authorities back to their country of origin. It added to the list of excluded aliens "persons suffering from a loathsome or dangerous contagious disease."

With these new regulations at his disposal, the first commissioner of Ellis Island, Colonel John B. Weber, welcomed the station's first immigrant, Annie Moore, on January 1, 1892. Immigration declined steadily in the course of the next five years, however, due in part to an epidemic of cholera (a severe intestinal disease) in Europe, and the new immigration station was rarely crowded. Then, on June 14, 1897, a fire erupted in one of the station buildings. Only an hour later, according to some accounts, the entire compound was in ashes. No one was hurt, but nearly all of the records detailing the arrivals of hundreds of thousands of immigrants in New York between the years 1855 and 1897 were lost in the blaze.

Immigration officials set up temporary operations at the barge office in lower Manhattan. Only a month later, builders began constructing a new fireproof station at Ellis Island. New York City sponsored a design contest to determine which architectural firm would win the construction job. The

On June 14, 1897, a fire broke out in the all-wooden building on Ellis Island, and it burned to the ground. The decision was made to rebuild the immigration center at the same location, but in the meantime a temporary office had to be opened. The barge office *(pictured here)* on the southeast tip of Manhattan, which briefly served as an immigration center in 1890–1891 after Castle Garden was shut down, was again pressed into service. It processed immigrant arrivals for more than three years until the new steel, brick, and stone buildings on Ellis Island opened on December 17, 1900.

winning design belonged to the architectural firm of Boring and Tilton, known mainly for its work on public libraries nationwide. The main building, of red brick with limestone trim, was to be situated at the center of the island. It would have a commanding presence, with three high-arched windows above the entrances on the east and west sides and spired towers at each corner. To the north of the main building would be the restaurant, laundry facility, bathhouse, and power plant. On a newly created island across from the ferry slip, a hospital would be built. These designs quickly became a reality, and the new station was completed in 1900, for a total cost of $1.5 million.

Immigration Scandals Continue

Though the new complex seemed to promise a fresh start for the United States's principal immigration center, from its first days, scandal plagued the new station at Ellis Island. Accusations quickly resurfaced that immigrants were being robbed, swindled, and abused by the station staff. In 1901, investigations revealed that steamship captains and immigration inspectors were selling fake U.S. citizenship papers to newly arrived immigrants, which would allow them to bypass inspection at Ellis Island. It was estimated that perhaps 10,000 people had entered New York in this way.

Later that year, President Theodore Roosevelt set about reforming the immigration machine at Ellis Island, beginning by hiring a new commissioner of immigration. Roosevelt chose a Wall Street lawyer named William Williams who introduced sweeping reforms at Ellis Island and shepherded the station through one of the most populous immigration waves in American history. Williams was a strict disciplinarian and insisted that the inspectors treat all of the immigrants with fairness and kindness. Under his supervision, inspectors no longer detained wealthy immigrants in the hopes of bribing them. Immigrants were no longer held in filthy detention rooms while they waited for medical examinations or board of inquiry hearings. Food sellers and money changers (people who exchanged the currency of an immigrant's native country for U.S. dollars) were no longer allowed to charge unfairly high fees for their goods and services.

Williams ushered in a new era at Ellis Island, one that was continued by his successor, Robert Watchorn. In the years that Williams and Watchorn ran the station, Ellis Island welcomed

This 1903 photograph shows President Theodore Roosevelt *(in glasses, second from right)* visiting Ellis Island. During his presidency, corruption was rampant at Ellis Island. Inspectors would demand bribes from immigrants. Railroad agents would sell tickets at inflated prices. Employees at the money exchange would charge a high exchange rate and keep the profits. Roosevelt was determined to end these practices. In April 1902, he appointed William Williams *(far right)*, a young Wall Street lawyer, as the new commissioner of Ellis Island. Williams began awarding food and baggage service contracts only to those companies that had good reputations. In addition, employees were constantly reminded to treat immigrants with kindness and care.

millions of these eager immigrants. In 1907, Ellis Island's busiest year, more than 1 million immigrants arrived at the station. Soon after it reopened, Ellis Island came to represent the gateway not only to New York and the country beyond, but also to the New World's promise of liberty and freedom.

CHAPTER 3

Between 1901 and 1914, when Ellis Island received its largest number of immigrant arrivals, Europe was in a state of turmoil. A large portion of the continent was divided into four autocratic empires (large states, each ruled by a single individual with absolute power). Germany was in the hands of Kaiser Wilhelm II. Czar Nicholas II ruled Russia. The Austro-Hungarian Empire was led by Emperor Franz Josef. Sultan Abdul Hamid II and his successor Sultan Mehmed V ruled the Ottoman Empire (based in modern-day Turkey).

THE JOURNEY

Each of these empires included multiethnic populations that practiced a number of different religions. Sometimes friction developed as a result. Religious persecution, economic depression, and political repression drove many Europeans to seek refuge in the United States. Some young men left Europe to avoid being drafted into the army, which in czarist Russia could require a commitment of up to twenty-five years' service. Many families came to America to escape the crippling poverty and food shortages typical of rural life in their eastern European villages. Thousands of Russian Jews fled pogroms—organized riots that left Jewish businesses and homes looted and burned, and thousands of Jews dead.

Immigrants often had to work day and night to save the money for the voyage. The trip itself might require traveling for months on foot or by wagon, train, boat, and ship, moving ever

At top left is an illustrated page from an 1891 edition of the magazine *Harper's Weekly* from an article about immigrants' arrivals at the immigration center in lower Manhattan's barge office. Italian, Swiss, Dutch, Hungarian, and Polish and Austrian Jews are all depicted. At bottom right is an advertisement printed by an Irish agency in the 1880s for transatlantic passage from Liverpool, England, to New York on ships of the White Star Line. The *Titanic*, which sank in 1912, was a White Star ship. For transcripts of the article and advertisement, see page 56.

westward toward America. At the turn of the century, an adult ticket on a transatlantic steamship cost about $35. Children were charged half that price, and infants traveled for free. Some immigrants borrowed the money from relatives. Others sold almost all of their belongings. Often, families were separated for years at a time so that fathers, husbands, and brothers could make a life in America, send money home to support their families, and save up for their relatives' eventual journeys to the United States.

Crossing the Atlantic

Though steamship companies often advertised a travel time of six days, the trip across the Atlantic could take anywhere from ten days to one month. Immigrants traveled in steerage, the lowest class of accommodations onboard. Deep in the hull of the ship, without portholes or decks, the immigrants were crowded into a single large room. A blanket hung over a rope divided the room down the center and separated the men from the women and children. The ceiling was only six or eight feet high.

Beds, stacked two or three high, lined the walls. Thin, lice-infested mattresses provided little comfort; those immigrants who traveled with their own feather bedding found the sleeping arrangements slightly more comfortable. Women with small children hoped to secure a lower bunk. These mothers slept with their arms around their children so that they would not fall to the floor as the boat rocked and swayed on the waves.

Directly beneath them, the ship's engines thundered day and night. There was virtually no ventilation, and bathroom facilities were inadequate. The stench of human waste was almost suffocating. There was little food, and the food that was offered, such as

This photograph shows steerage passengers enjoying a rare opportunity to breathe fresh air on deck during their transatlantic crossing to New York. Most steamships could carry as many as 2,000 passengers in steerage. The term "steerage" refers to the ship's lower decks where the steering mechanism of sailing ships had once been housed but now housed the impoverished travelers. These belowdecks compartments were densely crowded, smelly, and often filthy. Because most ships did not provide steerage passengers with a dining room of their own until after the turn of the century, the immigrants often ate their meals above deck in the open air.

soggy bread and cured fish, was often inedible. Prepared travelers brought their own supply of food, but more often than not, pangs of hunger went unanswered. During the day, the immigrants could enjoy fresh air on the upper decks. However, when the seas turned stormy, which they usually did at some point during the trip, the hatch to the lower deck was locked and tied, confining the steerage

This 1887 illustration captures the moment in which immigrants catch their first sight of the Statue of Liberty as their ship steams into New York Harbor. Between the opening of Castle Garden as an immigration center in 1855 through 1880, the majority of immigrants to the United States came from Ireland and Germany. Between 1880 and 1919, more than 23 million people immigrated to the United States. Almost three out of four of them entered through New York City. The two largest groups during this period were Russian Jews and Italians.

passengers to their dormitory-like room. Fresh water was available only on the upper deck, so during a storm the steerage passengers went without. Almost all passengers experienced severe seasickness. Many wondered if they would arrive in America alive.

Entering New York Harbor

Yet on that final day, when New York Harbor could be seen in the distance, the immigrants dressed themselves and their children in their best clothes, often bundling up in two or three coats so that they had less to carry. They crowded the deck of the steamship as the city and the Statue of Liberty came into view—their first glimpse of America!

The ship docked at a pier on the Hudson River, and the first- and second-class passengers (usually American citizens and wealthier new immigrants) enjoyed a relatively quick inspection onboard before debarking and dispersing to their destinations. Meanwhile, the steerage passengers waited onboard the steamship, sometimes for hours, before being transferred to the ferry that would take them to Ellis Island. Once they had crowded onto the ferry, however, it might not move from its mooring for hours. The immigrants, weighed down by layers of clothing, crying infants, and every kind of bulky luggage, were forced to stand on the open decks without food or water, wondering what would happen next.

As they waited, they gazed across the wide expanse of the Hudson River at Ellis Island. The station represented the last obstacle to freedom and the beginning of a new life in America. Many immigrants looked with dread on the imposing structure, wondering whether the golden door would be opened for them.

CHAPTER 4

WRUNG THROUGH THE MACHINE

The ferry deposited its cargo of weary new arrivals at the landing on Ellis Island. After such a long and exhausting journey, the welcome was often rougher and ruder than expected. The immigrants were herded off the ships and into lines, separated from family members, barked at by uniformed immigration officials, and occasionally swindled by dishonest porters, money changers, and corrupt immigration officials. As wearying as the months of preparation before departure had been, as difficult as the ocean crossing was, the first few hours or days on Ellis Island would often prove the hardest part of an immigrant's journey.

Passenger Manifests

According to legislation passed in 1893, steamship captains were required to provide passenger manifests, or lists, detailing the particulars of each immigrant, including marital status, occupation, final destination, and political affiliation (the political parties or organizations to which they belonged). Lawmakers believed that this policy would help reduce ticket sales at an immigrant's port of origin. Because steamship companies had to pay for the return voyages of rejected and deported immigrants, company ticket agents would conduct preliminary inspections when creating the manifests

While sailing to Europe on the luxury steamship *Kaiser Wilhelm II* in 1907, the photographer Alfred Stieglitz became interested in the many passengers crowded belowdecks in steerage. He became increasingly uncomfortable with the rich passengers with whom he crossed the Atlantic and was drawn to what he thought was the more natural simplicity of the steerage passengers. Upon arrival in Europe, he hurried off the ship to photograph the steerage passengers waiting to disembark. These men and women were actually "re-emigrants." Some estimates indicate that as many as 17 percent of immigrants eventually returned to their home countries. While the vast majority of Eastern Europeans, Irish, German, and Scandinavian immigrants stayed in the United States, roughly half of the Italian, Spanish, and Russian immigrants are thought to have eventually returned home.

and refuse to sell tickets to those immigrants who would almost certainly be rejected once they reached America.

As a result, all immigrants carried slips of paper bearing their manifest numbers, often pinned to their dresses or coats. Arranged in groups according to their manifest numbers, they passed under a crowded iron-and-glass canopy and through the doors of the main building.

The Medical Inspection

Herded up a staircase, the immigrants were next ushered through the medical inspection line. Most assumed that the medical inspection did not begin until they reached the doctor at the head of the line, but as the immigrants stood waiting, they were already being observed and screened by other doctors standing discreetly off to either side. The immigrants passed through a small railed maze that forced them to turn at right angles to the unnoticed examiners, allowing the doctors to observe the aliens from various angles. These doctors noted the way the immigrants walked, the quality of their complexions, and their general demeanors to try to identify any obvious signs of disease or disability.

Once the immigrants reached the examining doctor at the head of the long line, special attention was paid to their eyes, hands, and throat, parts of the body where infections could be developing and symptoms of illness could be detected. Trachoma, an eye disease, and favus, a skin disease, were common, contagious, and difficult to treat. Both diseases were grounds for immediate deportation. The immigrants were also given stamped identification cards, which each instinctively tried to read, thus giving the doctors the opportunity to test each immigrant's eyesight.

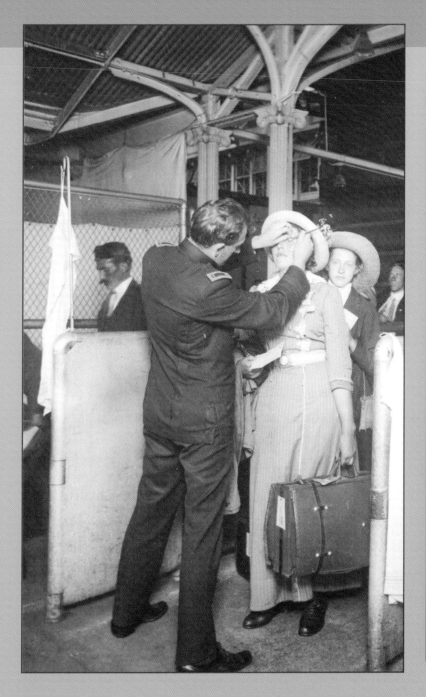

Chalk Markings

X	Suspected mental defect
⊗	Mental disease
B	Back
C	Conjunctivitis
CT	Trachoma
E	Eyes
F	Face
F+	Feet
G	Goiter
H	Heart
K	Hernia
L	Lameness
N	Neck
P	Physical/Lungs
Pg	Pregnancy
Sc	Scalp (Favus)
S	Senility

An immigrant being tested for the highly contagious eye infection trachoma is shown in the photograph at left. Because trachoma was so infectious and hard to cure, those with the infection were usually isolated and sent back to their home countries as soon as possible. At right is a list of symbols for diseases and ailments doctors looked for during their extremely brief examinations of immigrants. If symptoms of a disease were observed, the examiner would chalk the appropriate symbol on the immigrant's shoulder or lapel. Immigrants bearing these chalk marks would be removed from the inspection line and given a more thorough physical exam.

Those immigrants who were thought to have physical or mental deficiencies were herded into caged enclosures, their coats marked in code with chalk, indicating the reason for their detainment. An *E* indicated a problem related to the eyes, *H* meant heart trouble, and *X* indicated suspected mental illness. If immigrants were ill, they would be treated in one of the station's hospital units and detained during their convalescence. A board of inquiry would review their medical conditions and determine if they would be allowed to remain in the United States or be forced to return to their homelands.

The Immigration Inspectors

Having undergone the medical inspection, those immigrants found to be healthy joined the lines that led to the desks of the immigration inspectors. Here they might wait for hours before coming before the man who would decide their fate. The immigration inspectors spent about two minutes with each immigrant, asking a series of questions based on the information printed in the ship's manifest. Because immigrants had heard about this phase of the process from relatives and friends who had immigrated earlier, they were often prepared for these questions and were able to deliver well-rehearsed answers. In later years, inspectors also administered literacy tests in the immigrants' native languages.

The immigration inspector's examination was full of drama and anxiety for hopeful immigrants. When the inspector asked immigrants whether they had jobs awaiting them at their final destination, the temptation to answer "Yes" was strong. The immigrants instinctively wanted to demonstrate that they could support themselves and their families and would not become burdens to

At right is a September 10, 1923, letter from an acting inspector to the commissioner of Immigration in Seattle, Washington, regarding a Chinese immigrant who had successfully requested re-entry to the United States. The Act to Prohibit the Coming of Chinese Persons into the United States, referred to as the Geary Act, was passed in May 1892 and extended indefinitely in 1902. While it restricted most Chinese immigration, it did allow Chinese laborers working in the United States to travel to China and re-enter the country as long as they registered themselves and obtained a certificate proving their right to be in the country.

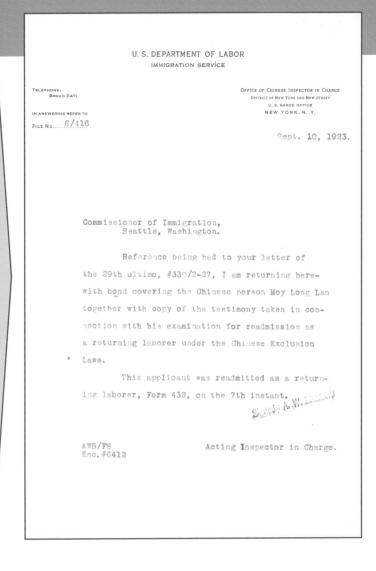

U. S. DEPARTMENT OF LABOR
IMMIGRATION SERVICE

TELEPHONE:
BROAD 3411

OFFICE OF CHINESE INSPECTOR IN CHARGE
DISTRICT OF NEW YORK AND NEW JERSEY
U. S. BARGE OFFICE
NEW YORK, N. Y.

IN ANSWERING REFER TO
FILE No. 6/416

Sept. 10, 1923.

Commissioner of Immigration,
Seattle, Washington.

Reference being had to your letter of the 29th ultimo, #330/3-37, I am returning herewith bond covering the Chinese person Moy Long Lan together with copy of the testimony taken in connection with his examination for readmission as a returning laborer under the Chinese Exclusion Laws.

This applicant was readmitted as a returning laborer, Form 432, on the 7th instant.

Signed: A.W. [illegible]

AWB/FS
Enc. #6412

Acting Inspector in Charge.

society. It was in their best interests to answer "No," however. Coming to America for the purpose of working for a specific employer on a specific job was in violation of the 1885 Alien Contract Labor Law. Somehow, immigrants had to prove that they did not have jobs already lined up, but that, if given the opportunity, they could find work easily and not become dependent on government aid soon after leaving Ellis Island.

The Detainees

Immigrants were detained for many reasons—personal, political, and economic. Those without money or immediate means to support themselves but with promises of aid from friends or relatives were often held until money was sent to them at the island or concerned relatives came to defend their application for entry. This was often the case for women and children whose husbands and fathers awaited them in the United States. If at the end of five days money or help had not arrived, poor and unsupported immigrants were given the choice of being deported or being turned over to the care of an American charitable organization.

If the government of an immigrant's native country warned U.S. officials that he or she was a convicted criminal, entry into the United States was denied. A member of a local labor union might inform immigration officials that an immigrant's journey had been paid for by his contracted employer, thereby violating the 1885 Alien Contract Labor Law. A deserted wife might alert authorities to the identity of her missing runaway husband. Inspectors also detained immigrants they suspected of being prostitutes, polygamists (men who have more than one wife), or supporters of certain unpopular or radical political views (such as Communism). Most often, however, immigrants were detained for one primary reason—money. Many were not permitted to leave the island and finally enter the United States until they could prove they would not become a public charge or dependent on private charity.

Having been declared unfit for entry, immigrants might return to their country of origin aboard the very ship on which they arrived in the United States. More often, however, they were held at Ellis Island for one or two weeks before another ship bound for their homeland made a scheduled departure. If they appealed the inspector's decision, they might enter into a lengthy legal proceeding, extending their stay at Ellis Island by weeks.

Detention on the island was often quite unpleasant, especially during the station's busiest years, between 1901 and 1914 (after which reforms greatly improved daily life for the internees). The aliens were crowded into locked dormitories or hospital wards. The dormitories were lice-infested and cramped, offering accommodations that immigrants compared unfavorably to Siberian prison camps and hell itself. The detainees met several times each day to enjoy hearty meals free of charge in the cafeteria-style dining halls but were otherwise left to entertain themselves. Families generally met only at meals, and the outdoors were enjoyed only on the tar-covered rooftops of the lower buildings.

About 20 percent of all arrivals were temporarily detained at Ellis Island. The rest were permitted to enter the country virtually without delay. Of those detained, only a small percentage was eventually excluded and deported. In 1914, for example, 878,052 immigrants were admitted at Ellis Island and 175,580 immigrants detained. Of the detainees, 16,588, or about 2 percent, were deported. Millions of immigrants walked past the desks of the immigration inspectors at Ellis Island. They continued on downstairs, where they met relatives or friends and boarded the ferry bound for lower Manhattan or the barges that would carry them to railroad stations in New Jersey.

Standing at the Threshold of America

Having overcome the obstacles of the medical inspection and immigration examination, immigrants finally stood before the open door of America. They were free to enter. As difficult as the journey that lay behind the immigrants was, what lay ahead, in cities and towns across America, was an even greater challenge: creating a new life in a foreign, bewildering land. Immigrants of all nationalities and from all walks of life faced discrimination and hostility. Many lived in squalor in the crowded tenements that

This photograph shows hundreds of immigrants standing in pens in the Great Hall of Ellis Island, waiting for the next stage of the processing procedure. Immigrants waited here for their interviews with legal inspectors after finishing their medical exams. If all went well, an immigrant could pass through Ellis Island and into the teeming streets of New York within three to five hours of arrival. Often, however, problems cropped up and entry was delayed. Some individuals and families stayed for days, weeks, and even months. The Great Hall is 200 feet long and 100 feet wide—nearly as large as two baseball fields. In 1918, it was used as an enormous hospital ward for American soldiers returning from World War I.

lined the streets of ethnic neighborhoods. Thousands labored long hours in the dangerous working conditions of the stock-yards and sweatshops of the major urban slums. Some fell victim to swindles, losing what little money they had to con men.

Many reacted to the anxieties of their new life by seeking comfort in their cultural traditions. They joined ethnic organizations, read foreign-language newspapers, and did not stray far from the neighborhoods where many of their former countrymen and countrywomen also lived. Others struggled to strike a balance between maintaining the traditions of their native culture and becoming active members of the larger American society. They would become assimilated—absorbed into the dynamic, multi-ethnic culture bubbling all around them. Their new status as American citizens would become at least as important to their identity as their ethnic heritage was.

Whether they kept to their own groups and traditions or embraced assimilation and a new American identity, the recently arrived immigrants continued to scrimp and save to pay for their relatives to join them in America. The stream of humanity continued to pour ceaselessly into New York Harbor, onto the shores of Ellis Island. Only the gales of two devastating world wars could stem its tide.

CHAPTER 5

THE TIDE BECOMES A TRICKLE

In the years leading up to 1914 and the outbreak of World War I, eastern and southern Europe had been the site of countless small battles between opposing empires. Young men were being called into service as the various European powers prepared for a full-scale war. Tensions mounted, and these local skirmishes came together in one worldwide conflict.

Closing the Gates

The beginning of the war in August 1914 reduced the immigrant traffic at Ellis Island to a trickle. The busiest emigration ports of Europe, such as Hamburg and Bremen in Germany, were blockaded by the British navy. Commercial traffic, including immigrant steamships, was chased from the high seas, where submarine warfare was fierce and civilian ships were threatened with attack. Those immigrants who wished to come to the United States could not, and those who had hoped to return to Europe after a few years in America were also disappointed. In 1915, Ellis Island saw only 178,416 new arrivals. This number continued to decline, reaching a low of 28,867 three years later.

In April 1917, the United States was finally drawn into World War I, three years after the conflict first broke out. Ellis Island was immediately transformed into a holding cell for 2,000

This November 1919 photograph shows suspected Communists getting out of a police wagon after being arrested during a raid in New York City. They are on their way to Ellis Island, where they would be detained until deportation proceedings decided whether they would be returned to their home countries. In 1919 and 1920, a wave of anti-Communist sentiment, known as the Red Scare, swept the United States. By June 1920, some 10,000 people had been arrested and imprisoned for their political beliefs or membership in certain labor and political organizations. About 800 of them were deported. The government's repression of radical movements involved coordinated raids from coast to coast. Men and women were rounded up, imprisoned without charges or access to a lawyer, and in some cases deported before their families could even learn their whereabouts.

German prisoners of war (POWs), primarily the crews of German ships moored in New York Harbor. The island was placed under military guard. A stockade (protective fence or enclosure) was built around the power plant to guard against sabotage. Floodlights were placed on all of the buildings to help prevent prisoner escapes.

As Ellis Island was being transformed into a POW camp, the federal Department of Justice and other smaller government agencies became increasingly aggressive in their efforts to deport resident aliens (noncitizens living legally in the United States) suspected of various crimes, especially those accused of being Communist sympathizers or revolutionaries. These people were labeled spies and saboteurs, and they were carefully guarded. Because there were no ships departing for Europe, however, these accused criminals had to be housed at Ellis Island with the German POWs.

In the spring of 1917, as the United States entered World War I, a new immigration law—the 1917 Immigration Act—went into effect. The law, which had been rejected by President Woodrow Wilson but revived when Congress overrode the president's veto, repealed all previous immigration legislation that was not in keeping with its detailed provisions. It specified thirty-two separate groups of undesirable immigrants, including among the excluded all those immigrants who could not read and write (adults, not children), the mentally challenged, alcoholics, epileptics, criminals, the handicapped, polygamists, revolutionaries, the impoverished, and the physically or mentally ill. The passage of this restrictive immigration law signaled to the world that America was closing its borders. Its gates were no longer opened wide for the world's immigrants.

With immigration to the U.S. increasingly restricted, Ellis Island's role changed and evolved. In 1918, the island's German POWs and accused alien criminals were transferred to internment camps elsewhere in the United States. The sick immigrants were turned over to private hospitals, and the medical facilities on the island were put in the hands of the army's medical department. The dormitories were turned into barracks and occupied by American soldiers. The bureau of immigration was required to do most of its inspections of new arrivals on the ships that had carried them across the Atlantic, not even allowing the immigrants to set foot on the island. Ellis Island—once the gateway to America for the world's hopeful masses—had been transformed into a military headquarters with the primary purpose of keeping people out.

Anti-Immigrant Sentiment and the Red Scare

With the end of World War I, Europe was transformed. Its once mighty imperial armies had been ravaged by war, and many people lived in extreme poverty. Its borders had been radically redrawn, and its old regimes had been toppled. This state of chaos and uncertainty made the United States a desirable destination once again, and interest in immigration increased.

Americans' interest in welcoming immigrants, however, had greatly decreased. Though the war had been fought on European soil, Americans, too, had lost sons and husbands in the conflict and had experienced the sacrifices of wartime shortages. Many Americans came to distrust foreigners and radicals, whom they blamed for the recent war. In large numbers, Americans turned their attention to the enemy that might be lurking in their own backyard, the democracy-hating revolutionary who was suspected

This is a circa 1905 photograph of women and children eating a meal in the dining hall of Ellis Island. Free meals were provided for the duration of an immigrant's stay at Ellis Island. Surviving menus show that bread, butter, crackers, milk, and coffee were provided for breakfast. Lunch might feature beef stew, boiled potatoes, and rye bread. A light dinner might include stewed prunes, baked beans, crackers, and tea. Kosher food was provided for Jewish immigrants, and other religion-based dietary restrictions were sometimes accommodated.

of trying to turn America into a Communist society. In the coming year, a series of labor strikes and random bombings, incorrectly blamed on Communist radicals, fueled their fear and anger.

Just weeks before the November 11, 1918, armistice (a truce) that put an end to fighting in Europe, Congress passed legislation that made it much easier to deport any resident alien suspected of being an anarchist (someone interested in overthrowing the government) or a Communist. A public

This political cartoon by John T. McCutcheon of the *Chicago Tribune* illustrates the growing anti-immigrant sentiment that took hold in Depression-era America. As thousands of "undesirable immigrants" flood off a docked ship to "steal" low-paying jobs in the city, they are confronted by the "American Army of the Unemployed." A poster above them proclaims the high unemployment rate among American citizens.

hysteria, known as the Red Scare (red was the color associated with Communist revolution), gripped the country, and over the next year many accused radicals were deported. The army and navy evacuated Ellis Island in 1919, and the station prepared to handle the outgoing flood of suspected "Reds." Mass deportations of suspected revolutionaries followed, with many of the detainees passing through Ellis Island on their way back to Europe.

In time, the Red Scare subsided, though it would resurface again in the late 1940s and gain great strength in the 1950s with the beginning of the Cold War between the United States and the Soviet Union. During the lull, however, Ellis Island returned to the business of processing new arrivals.

By 1920, the number of new arrivals was again on the rise. Ellis Island welcomed 225,206 immigrants that year. Once again, New York harbor was crowded with arrivals, and passengers had to wait for hours to be ferried to the island and examined in the registry hall. The dining halls, meant to seat 800 each, were again crowded with 3,000 people in each hall at every meal. This overcrowding was in part due to the fact that the immigrants were given more rigorous and time-consuming examinations, as required under the 1917 Immigration Act. Literacy tests were administered. Each immigrant also received an extensive medical exam. Throughout this period, all arrivals were deloused to protect against typhus, a severe bacterial disease carried by body lice and causing fever, rash, headaches, and delirium. Their baggage and clothes were also taken from them to be disinfected as a precaution.

As if the rigorous and often humiliating screenings and examinations were not difficult enough on the immigrants, the facilities on Ellis Island were falling into severe disrepair. Most observers agreed that the living quarters were filthy, cramped, and infested with vermin, such as rats and lice. The island was extremely under-staffed, employees were overworked, and the immigrants, who were mostly very poor war refugees, were often mistreated. They slept on blankets laid on the floor because there were never enough beds. They were herded like animals from one room to the next and denied any kind of privacy. The buildings themselves, which had seen the comings and goings of millions of new Americans over their twenty-year history, were crumbling.

Fear Leads to Quotas

With the sudden increase in immigration levels in the early 1920s, the voices of those in favor of stricter immigration policies were once again heard. The beginning of an economic recession

Union Calendar No. 2.

67TH CONGRESS,
1ST SESSION.

H. R. 4075.

[Report No. 4.]

IN THE HOUSE OF REPRESENTATIVES.

APRIL 18, 1921.

Mr. JOHNSON of Washington introduced the following bill; which was referred to the Committee on Immigration and Naturalization and ordered to be printed.

APRIL 19, 1921.

Reported with amendments, committed to the Committee of the Whole House on the state of the Union, and ordered to be printed.

[Omit the part struck through and insert the part printed in italic.]

A BILL

To limit the immigration of aliens into the United States.

1   Be it enacted by the Senate and House of Representa-

2   tives of the United States of America in Congress assembled,

3   That as used in this Act—

4   The term "United States" means the United States

Amendment offered by Mr. _____

Page ___, *line* ___

After the word _____

Strike out
Insert

After the end of World War I, a huge influx of immigrants from southern and eastern Europe led many Americans to support restrictive immigration laws. Responding to this pressure, Congress passed the First Quota Act. A desk copy of the House of Representatives bill that, once passed, would become the Quota Act appears above. This act limited the number of immigrants from each nation allowed into the United States each year to 3 percent of that nationality's presence in the U.S. population as recorded by the 1910 census. No more than 350,000 immigrants total would be allowed to enter the country each year. As a result, immigration from southern and eastern Europe dropped to less than one-quarter of its pre–World War I levels. An even more restrictive quota act was passed six years later, restricting total immigration to 150,000 lucky individuals. This would remain in effect through the mid-1960s. For a transcription of the First Quota Act, see page 57.

early in the decade roused the Knights of Labor again to demand stricter controls. The postwar European typhus epidemic was another cause for concern among several influential health commissioners. In response, the House of Representatives proposed suspending immigration for one year. No new aliens would be allowed to enter while the government worked out a plan for dealing with the increasing numbers of people seeking refuge in America. In the end, both houses of Congress enacted what has come to be called the First Quota Act, effective June 3, 1921.

The First Quota Act was intended as a temporary solution to the country's immigration woes, but it soon became the basis for American immigration law until 1965. The law stated that each foreign country would be allowed only a certain number of emigrants to be admitted to the United States. Each country's quota would be set at 3 percent of the population of that nationality living in the United States during the 1910 census. For example, the number of Italians admitted to the United States in 1923 could not exceed 3 percent of the number of foreign-born Italians living in the United States in 1910. In addition, the quota was spread out over the year, so that no more than 20 percent of the annual quota could be admitted in any given month. Finally, the law said that the total number of immigrants admitted to the United States in a single year under the quota system would not exceed 358,000. Once that number of immigrants had arrived in the United States, all immigration for that year would cease, even if foreign countries had not yet reached their quota. Given that more than 1 million immigrants used to be admitted every year, these regulations dealt a crushing blow to thousands of hopeful emigrants.

In the spring of 1924, Congress passed the Second Quota Act, which was to go into effect the following year. The new law set

This May 1923 photograph shows a boat of immigrants sailing away from the dock at Ellis Island back to ships that would return them to Europe and their home countries. Their applications for admission into the United States had been rejected under the First Quota Act. Under the provisions of the First and Second Quota Acts, roughly 70 percent of all immigrant slots were allotted to natives of just three countries—the United Kingdom, Ireland, and Germany. Many of these quotas went unfilled, as immigration from these countries slowed in the twentieth century. There were long waiting lists, however, for the small number of visas available to those born in Italy, Greece, Poland, Portugal, and elsewhere in eastern and southern Europe.

each foreign nation's quota at 2 percent of the population of its former citizens living in the United States in 1890, further reducing the potential number of admitted immigrants. It also set the total number of admitted aliens per year at 164,000, down from 358,000. Finally, and most importantly, the law required European immigrants to obtain visas from the American consuls located in their countries of origin. To do so involved undergoing a thorough examination akin to those performed at Ellis Island. This measure was intended to prevent "undesirable" immigrants—particulary southern Europeans—from spending their time and money to make the transatlantic voyage only to be rejected by the inspectors at Ellis Island. The Second Quota Act served its purpose; immigration at Ellis Island was sharply reduced. On an average day following its enactment, only 300 immigrants arrived at the station.

Shortly after the law took effect, the surgeon general of the United States suggested employing medical examiners at all of the U.S. consulates overseas to further curb the rate of immigrants who were deported for medical reasons. This was done, and the examiners performed thorough exams on all potential immigrants before visas were issued. Eventually, immigration inspectors were added to the staffs of overseas consulates, ensuring that all transatlantic passengers were "pre-processed" before reaching Ellis Island. Under this new system, a visa came to guarantee entrance into the United States.

As a result, the primary function of immigration stations such as Ellis Island—to review immigrants and determine whether they should be admitted—was made unnecessary. All of the screening was taking place at an immigrant's point of departure—his or her home country—rather than in an immigration station in the United States.

Twilight Falls on Ellis Island

By 1928, Ellis Island was viewed by many as a hulking, expensive, obsolete institution. Yet it remained in service, even during the darkest hours of the stock market crash of 1929 and the prolonged Depression that followed throughout the 1930s. Because the United States was suffering such a severe economic crisis, to foreigners it no longer looked like the land of opportunity.

Ellis Island was closed and vacated on November 12, 1954. In this photograph, an employee who had worked at the immigration center for thirty years waves goodbye as the very last ferry sails away from the island. Ellis Island had processed immigrants for sixty-two years, but would become a shuttered ruin for more than thirty years after its closing. A refurbished Ellis Island reopened as an immigration museum in 1990. In 1998, the U.S. Supreme Court ruled that Ellis Island actually fell within the borders of New Jersey, not New York. Though the federal government owns the island, most of it is now designated as belonging within New Jersey.

During this period, immigration was nearly nonexistent. So Ellis Island began to be used mainly as a deportation center, as the Justice Department and other federal agencies focused on expelling illegal aliens. Other foreign-born residents left gladly, at the government's expense, to escape the desperate economic conditions facing America.

Meanwhile, in Europe, totalitarian regimes were again taking hold. Though a strong minority of voices spoke up in favor of offering American refuge to German and Austrian Jews living under Adolf Hitler's Third Reich, the anti-immigration faction in Congress defeated proposals to loosen entry laws. In 1940, the Nazis invaded Norway and France. In response, the U.S. State Department, afraid Nazi spies would infiltrate America disguised as refugees, ordered American consulates overseas to tighten their restrictions on visas. All told, perhaps only 250,000 European refugees seeking asylum were admitted to the United States during World War II.

By the late 1930s, the immigrant had ceased to be viewed as an imported good, a potential labor force, or a charity case. As the United States prepared to enter World War II, the immigrant was viewed only as a threat to national security. The Alien Registration Act of June 1940 required all resident aliens to be registered and all arriving immigrants to be fingerprinted. During the war, Ellis Island—in particular the baggage and dormitory building—once again served as a detention center for seamen from enemy nations and suspected foreign-born criminals. The U.S. Coast Guard also used the island as a training center.

Following the end of World War II, Ellis Island would see a final flurry of immigration activity in 1950—mostly the processing and housing of detainees and deportees—with the passage of the Internal Security Act, which excluded members of Communist and Fascist organizations from entering the United States. Though the Immigration and Naturalization Service would continue to occupy the buildings until 1955, Ellis Island no longer functioned as a working immigration station in its final postwar years. Having processed 12 million immigrants from 1892 to 1954, Ellis Island was closing its dilapidated doors.

In November 1954, the island was vacated, the last immigration authorities were relocated to their new offices on Manhattan's Columbus Avenue, and the Ellis Island ferry became permanently moored in its slip.

CHAPTER 6

ELLIS ISLAND REBORN

After its closing, Ellis Island lay abandoned for many years. During this time, with only a lone caretaker and his bulldog left to guard the island, the buildings fell into severe disrepair. Paint peeled in large sheets from the walls. Water-damaged ceilings buckled. Weeds grew up all over the island. Birds made nests in the upper stories of the once grand buildings. Thieves visited the island at night and stole abandoned furniture and supplies. Just a few hundred yards from the sleek bustle of Manhattan, one of the most valuable and important sites of American history was left to ruin.

When the nation again turned its attention to the crumbling structures, various proposals were made to turn the island into a park and recreation center, a resort, a home for the elderly, an alcohol rehabilitation center, and even a liberal arts college. These recommendations were eventually all rejected. Instead, on May 11, 1965, President Lyndon B. Johnson declared that Ellis Island would become part of the Statue of Liberty National Monument, operated by the National Park Service. During the ceremony that unveiled this plan, Johnson also announced the terms of his proposed immigration bill, which would repeal the anti-immigration policies of the First and Second Quota Acts.

This is a photograph of the restored Great Hall of Ellis Island, which is now part of the Ellis Island Immigration Museum. In 1965, Ellis Island became part of the National Park Service, paving the way for its eventual restoration. It was not until 1974, however, that the Restore Ellis Island Committee was formed to raise funds for renovation. Finally, in 1983, restoration of the main building began. After a six-year, $162 million renovation, Ellis Island reopened to the public as a museum in 1990. Two years later, Ellis Island celebrated its centennial. In 1999, Congress authorized the spending of $8.6 million to begin renovating more than thirty other buildings on Ellis Island, including ferry, hospital buildings, and laundry buildings.

Between 1976 and 1984, Ellis Island was open to the public on a limited basis. During this time, an in-depth study of the history of the immigration station was made, and architectural proposals for its renovation were presented. In 1984, after nearly twenty years of debate and disagreement, the island was temporarily closed to the public, and the massive reconstruction project began. After six years and $162 million dollars worth of careful restoration, the Ellis Island Immigration Museum—housed in the former main building—was opened to the public on September 10, 1990. The structure was restored to look as it did between 1918 and 1924. The iron-and-glass canopy was redesigned with modern influences and a restaurant patio was added, but the structures were otherwise restored to all of their former glory.

Various exhibits document the role Ellis Island played in the immigrant experience and offer a larger view of the 400-year history of immigration to America. The museum includes personal objects and artifacts, vintage desks and benches, documents, photographs, documentary films, historical reenactments of actual hearings for arrivals who failed inspection, and the oral histories of immigrants who passed through Ellis Island. An American Immigrant Wall of Honor lists the names of more than 600,000 individuals who immigrated to America, and more names are regularly added. The museum also features the American Family Immigration History Center, a research facility that contains ships' records for more than 22 million people who passed through Ellis Island from 1892 to 1924. The various exhibits and research library are housed in the center's former baggage room, railroad ticket office, registry room, great hall, dormitory, and hearing rooms.

A young girl searches for the name of one of her ancestors on the American Immigrant Wall of Honor at Ellis Island. The wall records the names of more than 500,000 individuals and families who left their homes to begin a new life in the New World. Famous names include George Washington's great-grandfather, Plymouth Plantation settlers Myles Standish and Priscilla Alden, the great-grandparents of John F. Kennedy, and the families of Gregory Peck, Cicely Tyson, Jay Leno, and Barbra Streisand. From this monument is a view of both the Statue of Liberty and the Manhattan skyline.

A trip to the Ellis Island Immigration Museum is an extraordinary experience, one that almost 2 million visitors per year enjoy. Because the vast majority of Americans are descended from immigrants or are immigrants themselves, the museum offers a unique connection to America's shared past. It allows visitors to both explore their own family histories and achieve a greater appreciation for the experiences of their fellow citizens. It provokes the realization in viewers that, regardless of how many generations their families have lived in the United States, they are almost certainly related to someone who was a bewildered newcomer, a frightened and hopeful foreigner, just looking for the opportunity to make a life for himself or herself in a free country.

Fear, hope, opportunity, and freedom—these make up the typical immigrant's story, and it is a tale that continues to unfold day after day in the United States. Every year, thousands of foreign-born citizens are given the opportunity to find refuge, opportunity, freedom, and prosperity in the United States. The heated debate over immigration policy rages on, as well. There will probably always be a large number of Americans who oppose the influx of foreigners, while an almost equal number of Americans will feel it is the nation's solemn duty to provide a home to the oppressed and downtrodden. This disagreement is unlikely to be resolved, and the country's immigration policies will probably continue to swing back and forth between these two sentiments.

Yet those who pay a visit to Ellis Island and its history are likely to be overwhelmed with gratitude that their ancestors were given the chance to become Americans. They will gain new respect and admiration for the brave individuals who continue to leave their homes and strike out into the unknown, in search of a better future for themselves and their families.

PRIMARY SOURCE TRANSCRIPTIONS

Page 23: Excerpt from an Article Appearing in the October 24, 1891, Issue of *Harper's Weekly*

Transcription

. . . The baggage of the immigrants had all been examined, "for revenue only," on the steamer at her wharf. It was now removed to the ground-floor of the Barge Office. A stranger to the ways of those who seek our shores would never dream to look at half of it, that the stuff they bring is baggage. The dubious moiety of it consists of bags and pudding-shaped bundles, almost always done up in what once was white or light-colored cloth, but which has become stained and grimed with handling and with the soot of soft-coal smoke. The trunks, when they have them, are not like our trunks. Some are made of tin, others are clumsy chests, and still others are covered with cow-skin, "with the hairy side out," or are painted like an Indian on the war path. As a rule, the swelling bundles that look like over-grown contain bedding, which the poor people have been obliged to buy, and do not want to lose.

As fast as a man or a woman left the boat, he or she went up to the Barge Office, to pass down one of two runways, or aisles, between railings, and to be questioned again by the upstairs inspectors, who desired to know their names, nationalities, ages; whether they were married or single; the number in each family; whither they were travelling, and if they had money or tickets with which to travel; whether they were ever inmates of an asylum or prison; their condition of health, their occupation, and whether they were citizens or aliens.

After all the immigrants had passed their examinations (under the eyes of the doctors, who singled several out for further inspection and questioning), the people who meant to remain in New York were assembled in a great pen, and the others were led to the barge, which is kept for lack of other room, in which the railway travellers are held until evening, when the barge is taken to meet the emigrant trains that are always started at night. Those who were permitted to enter the country were then at liberty to ask questions at the information bureau; to wire their friends from the "telegraphen bureau," or "telegraphen contor," as it was variously called; or to have their money changed at the desk of Mr. E. W. Austin, the official broker . . . There is a lunch counter, also, in the Barge Office, and on it are to be seen bottles of beer, sandwiches made of junks of rye-bread, capped by great lengths of sausage, and pie, and crullers. When a prosperous looking Hollander was asked why he did not eat butter on his bread, he replied that he was not used to it; that he made a great deal of it every year, but sold it all, and never dreamed of eating it.

Page 23: Excerpt from a c. 1880 White Star Line Advertisement for Passage from Liverpool to New York

Transcription

. . . The steerage accommodation in these Steamers is of the very highest character, the rooms are unusually spacious, well-lighted, ventilated, and warmed, and passengers of this class will find their comfort carefully studied. Passengers will be provided with Berths to sleep in, each adult having a separate berth; but they have to provide themselves with a Plate, Mug, Knife, Fork, Spoon, and Water Can, also Bedding,—all of which can be purchased on shore . . . MARRIED COUPLES, WITH THEIR CHILDREN, WILL BE BERTHED TOGETHER. FEMALES will be Berthed in rooms by themselves.

BILL OF FARE.—Each passenger will be supplied with 3 quarts of Water daily, and with as much Provisions as he can eat, which are all of the best quality, and which are examined and put on board under the inspection of Her Majesty's Emigration Officers, and cooked and served by the Company's servants.

BREAKFAST AT EIGHT O'CLOCK.—Coffee, Sugar, and fresh Bread and Butter, or Biscuit and Butter, or Oatmeal Porridge and Molasses.

DINNER AT ONE O'CLOCK.—Soup and Beef, Pork, or Fish, according to the day of the week, with Bread and Potatoes, and on Sunday Pudding will be added.

SUPPER AT SIX O'CLOCK.—Tea, Sugar, Biscuit, and Butter. Oatmeal Gruel will be supplied at 8 p.m. when necessary.

All passengers are liable to be rejected, who, upon examination, are found to be lunatic, idiot, deaf, dumb, blind, maimed, or infirm, or above the age of 60 years; or widow with a child or children; or any woman without a husband with a child or children; or any person unable to take care of himself (or herself) without becoming a public charge, or who from any attending circumstances are likely to become a public charge, or who from sickness or disease, existing at the time of departure, are likely soon to become a public charge. Sick persons or widows with children cannot be taken, nor lame persons, unless full security be given for the Bonds to be entered into by the Steamer to the United States Government, that the parties will not become chargeable to the State. . . .

AN EXPERIENCED SURGEON IS CARRIED BY EACH STEAMER. STEWARDESSES IN STEERAGE TO ATTEND THE WOMEN AND CHILDREN. NO FEES OR EXTRA CHARGES. . . .

Page 45: Excerpt from a Desk Copy of the Bill Presented in the House of Representatives on April 18, 1921, That Resulted in the First Quota Act.

Transcription

IN THE HOUSE OF REPRESENTATIVES.

April 18, 1921.

Mr. Johnson of Washington introduced the following bill; which was referred to the Committee on Immigration and Naturalization and ordered to be printed.

A BILL

To limit the immigration of aliens into the United States.

Be it enacted by the Senate and House of Representatives of the United States of America in Congress assembled, That as used in this Act—

The term "United States" means the United States, and any waters, territory, or other place subject to the jurisdiction thereof except the Canal Zone and the Philippine Islands; but if any alien leaves the Canal Zone or any insular possession of the United States and attempts to enter any other place under the jurisdiction of the United States nothing contained in this Act shall be construed as permitting him to enter under any other conditions than those applicable to all aliens.

The word "alien" includes any person not a native-born or naturalized citizen of the United States, but this definition shall not be held to include Indians of the United States not taxed nor citizens of the islands under the jurisdiction of the United States.

The term "Immigration Act" means the Act of February 5, 1917, entitled "An Act to regulate the immigration of aliens to, and the residence of aliens in, the United States"; and the term "immigration laws" includes such Act and all laws, conventions, and treaties of the United States relating to the immigration, exclusion, or expulsion of aliens.

Sec. 2. (a) That the number of aliens of any nationality who may be admitted under the immigration laws to the United States in any fiscal year shall be limited to 3 per centum of the number of foreign born persons of such nationality resident in the United States as determined by the United States census of 1910. . . .

GLOSSARY

affiliation One's connection to someone or something.

alien A foreign-born person.

anarchist A person who rebels against a ruling power or established authority.

armistice An end to war agreed upon by the opposing sides.

assimilate To adopt the culture of the majority of people in a society.

asylum A place of refuge or shelter.

autocracy A government in which one person holds absolute power.

battery A grouping of large guns for defensive purposes.

charge A person who is supported financially by the state and local government.

cholera An often deadly intestinal disease.

Communists In Russia, members of the Social Democratic Party, or someone advocating the elimination of private property.

consulate The office of officials sent to a foreign country as representatives of their country of origin.

convalescence Period of recovery from illness or injury.

dilapidated Broken-down.

dredge To remove earth from an ocean floor or river bottom to create a deeper channel.

fortifications Defensive works.

garrison A military post.

nativist Someone who prefers native inhabitants to immigrants.

polygamist Someone who is married to two or more people simultaneously.

saboteur Person who intentionally destroys property in an effort to disable a country's war effort.

visa Document that verifies one's approval or endorsement by the country one wishes to enter.

FOR MORE INFORMATION

Ellis Island Immigration Museum
Aramark Sports and Entertainment, Inc.
New York, NY 10004
Web site: http://www.ellisisland.com

The Immigration and Naturalization Service (INS)
425 I Street NW
Washington, DC 20536
Web site: http://www.bcis.gov/graphics/index.htm

The Statue of Liberty—Ellis Island Foundation, Inc.
Attn: American Family Immigration History Center
292 Madison Avenue
New York, NY 10017
Web site: http://www.ellisisland.org

Web Sites
Due to the changing nature of Internet links, the Rosen Publishing
Group, Inc., has developed an online list of Web sites related to the
subject of this book. This site is updated regularly. Please use this
link to access the list:

http://www.rosenlinks.com/psah/elis

FOR FURTHER READING

Bierman, Carol. *Journey to Ellis Island*. New York: Hyperion Press, 1998.

Coan, Peter Morton. *Ellis Island Interviews*. New York: Checkmark Books, 1998.

Colletta, John Philip, Ph.D. *They Came in Ships*. Salt Lake City: Ancestry Publishing, 2002.

Jacobs, William Jay. *Ellis Island: New Hope in a New Land*. New York: Atheneum, 1990.

Lawlor, Veronica, ed. *I Was Dreaming to Come to America: Memories from the Ellis Island Oral History Project*. New York: Scott Foresman, 1997.

Levine, Ellen. *If Your Name Was Changed at Ellis Island*. New York: Scholastic, 1994.

Szucs, Loretto Dennis. *Ellis Island: Tracing Your Family History Through America's Gateway*. Salt Lake City: Ancestry Publishing, 2001.

# BIBLIOGRAPHY

Anbinder, Tyler. *Five Points*. New York: The Free Press, 2001.

Briggs, Vernon M., Jr. *Mass Immigration and the National Interest*. Armonk, NY: M. E. Sharpe, Inc., 1992.

Brownstone, David M., Irene Franck, and Douglass L. Brownstone. *Island of Hope, Island of Tears*. New York: Metro Books, 2002.

Daniels, Roger. *Coming to America: A History of Immigration and Ethnicity in American Life*. New York: Perennial, 2002.

Dinnerstein, Leonard, and David M. Reimers. *Ethnic Americans*. New York: Columbia University Press, 1999.

Jonas, Susan, ed. *Ellis Island: Echoes from a Nation's Past*. New York: Aperture Foundation, 1997.

Pitkin, Thomas Monroe. *Keepers of the Gate*. New York: New York University Press, 1975.

Riis, Jacob A. *How the Other Half Lives: Studies Among the Tenements of New York*. New York: Penguin USA, 1997.

Takaki, Ronald T. *A Different Mirror: A History of Multicultural America*. Boston: Little, Brown & Co., 1994.

PRIMARY SOURCE IMAGE LIST

Page 5: A postcard featuring a photograph of Ellis Island by Irving Underhill. Published by the Manhattan Post Card Company.

Page 9: A 1664 map by an anonymous cartographer entitled *The Duke's Plan: A Description of the Towne of Mannados or New Amsterdam.* Based on a 1661 map made for Dutch authorities by Jacques Cortelyou. Courtesy of the New York Public Library.

Page 11: A sketch by Theodore R. Davis of Fort Gibson and the Naval Magazine on Ellis Island, published in the March 14, 1868, edition of *Harper's Weekly.* Courtesy of Corbis.

Page 13: A c. 1869 print entitled *Castle Garden, Landing for Emigrants, Barge Office, Battery,* first published by Charles Magnus. Courtesy of the New York Public Library.

Page 17 (top): A sketch dated October 24, 1891, by J. O. Davidson entitled *Ellis Island Immigrant Building.* Based on a photograph by J. U. Stead. Courtesy of the New York Public Library.

Page 17 (bottom): An untitled June 13, 1907, photograph of construction workers at Ellis Island. Housed in the National Archives.

Page 19: A c. 1870 stereograph of the Barge Office, photographer unknown. Housed in the New York Historical Society.

Page 21: An 1803 photograph of President Theodore Roosevelt and Immigration Commissioner William Williams. Photographer unknown. Housed in the William Williams Collection of the New York Public Library.

Page 23 (top left): Illustrations of immigrants from various countries from an article appearing in the October 24, 1891, issue of *Harper's Weekly.* Courtesy of the New York Public Library.

Page 23 (bottom right): A White Star Line advertisement printed by an Irish travel agency in the 1880s.

Page 25: A c. 1890 photograph by William H. Rau of steerage passengers on deck. Courtesy of the Library of Congress.

Page 26: An 1887 print entitled *New York: Welcome to the Land of Freedom.* Courtesy of the Library of Congress.

Page 29: A 1907 photograph by Alfred Stieglitz entitled *The Steerage.* Courtesy of the Library of Congress.

Page 33: A letter from the Acting Inspector in Charge to the Commissioner of Immigration in Seattle, Washington, concerning the readmission into the U.S. of Chinese citizen Moy Long Lam. Dated September 10, 1923. Housed in the National Archives and Records Administration.

Page 36: An undated photograph of the Great Hall of Ellis Island. Courtesy of the Associated Press and the National Parks Service.

Page 39: A November 8, 1919, photograph entitled *Reds and Bolsheviks Pending Deportation.* Courtesy of Bettmann/CORBIS.

Page 42: A c. 1905 photograph of women and children eating a meal in the dining hall of Ellis Island. Housed in the New York Public Library.

Page 43: A c. 1930 political cartoon by John T. McCutcheon that first appeared in the *Chicago Tribune.* Courtesy of the National Park Service.

Page 45: A desk copy of the bill presented in the House of Representatives on April 18, 1921, that once passed would become the First Quota Act. Housed in the Legislative Archives.

Page 47: A May 2, 1923, photograph entitled *Immigrants Rejected into United States.* Courtesy of Bettmann/CORBIS.

Page 49: A November 12, 1954, photograph entitled *Lone Man Standing and Gazing at Ellis Island.* Courtesy of Bettmann/CORBIS.

INDEX

About the Author

Gillian Houghton is an editor and freelance writer in New York City.

Photo Credits

Front cover, back cover (top left and bottom right), pp. 26, 29 Library of Congress, Prints and Photographs Division; back cover (top right) National Park Service, artist, Keith Rocco; back cover (middle left) Yale Collection of Western Americana, Beinecke Rare Book and Manuscript Library; back cover (middle right) Louisiana State Museum, Gift of Dr. and Mrs. E. Ralph Lupin; back cover (bottom left) Woolaroc Museum, Bartlesville, Oklahoma; pp. 1, 39, 47, 49 © Bettmann/Corbis; pp. 5, 19 Collection of The New-York Historical Society; pp. 9, 13, 17 (top), 23 (left), 36, 42 Picture Collection, The Branch Libraries, The New York Public Library, Astor, Lenox, and Tilden Foundations; pp. 11, 52 © Corbis; pp. 17 (bottom), 31 (left), 33 National Archives and Records Administration; pp. 21, 23 (right), 25, 31 (right), 43 Courtesy National Park Service, Statue of Liberty National Monument; p. 45 Records of the U.S. House of Representatives, National Archives and Records Administration; p. 54 Ted Horowitz/Corbis.

Designer: **Nelson Sa**; Photo Researcher: Amy Feinberg

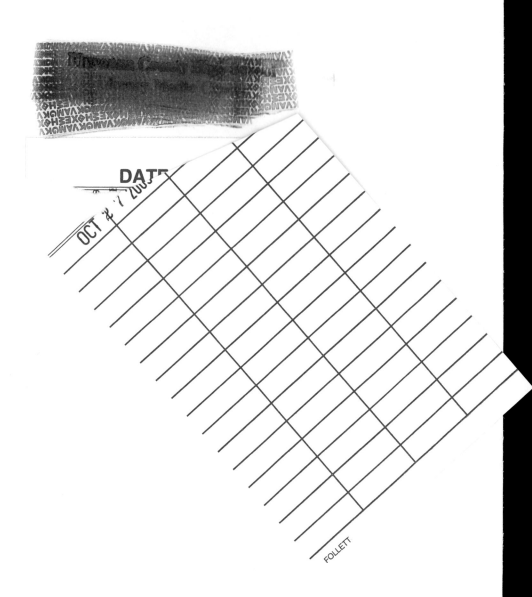

DATE

OCT 2 7 2003

FOLLETT